THE PUPPY PLACE

SPIRIT

SPIRIT

ELLEN
MILES

SCHOLASTIC INC.

Special thanks to Kristin Earhart

ISBN 978-1-338-21265-5

10 9 8 7 6 5 4   18 19 20 21 22

Printed in the U.S.A.   40

First printing 2018

CHAPTER ONE

Brrrrr!

Lizzie Peterson pulled her hood up over her red wool winter hat. It hadn't seemed so cold when she left her house, but that was before the wind had picked up. Now, it was fierce. The brisk gusts blew snow from the trees. Icy crystals prickled at Lizzie's face. *Brrrrr!*

Lizzie usually loved snow. When it was light and fluffy, it was perfect for playing with Buddy, her family's sweet, funny puppy. In fresh snow, Buddy would leap around, chasing and biting at snowballs. It made Lizzie and her younger brothers, Charles and the Bean, laugh out loud every time. Whenever the puppy managed to catch a clump of snow, he would immediately drop it and shake his head. The snow was just too cold for Buddy's mouth!

Today's snow was not light or fluffy. It was more like hail, hard little balls of ice. It left a shiny, crunchy layer on the snow from the day before. If the weather tomorrow was nicer, Lizzie would play outside with Buddy. Today, she had other plans. She was going to her friend Mariko's house.

Lizzie had met Mariko in the Greenies, an environmental club. Last summer, Lizzie and Mariko had gone wild blueberry picking along with Lizzie's best friend, Maria. Together, the three girls had filled two big buckets with the plump, ink-colored berries. They finished up with a lot of blueberries, even though they all admitted to sneaking some bites as they picked. Afterward they baked blueberry muffins at Mariko's house. It had been so much fun. Lizzie remembered how delicious the whole house had smelled. She had imagined she was a character in *Blueberries for Sal*, which was one of the Bean's favorite books.

Lizzie was excited for today, too. Mariko had invited her to make maple syrup candy, from real maple syrup. It sounded like something Lizzie — and her sweet tooth — would really enjoy. The only downside was that Maria couldn't be there. Maria was training for a big indoor horse show, so she was busy for the next few weekends.

Lizzie adjusted her scarf to cover her nose and mouth. It was so cold! Plus, it had started to hail again — icy pellets that pinged off Lizzie's jacket and stung her forehead. Even though she had gloves on, Lizzie shoved her hands into her pockets. She tried to walk faster, but the crusty snow was deep and hard to push through. Even though it would have been much warmer to ride over in the car with Dad, Lizzie had really wanted to walk to Mariko's today. She had pictured a snowy adventure, but this was turning out to be a lot snowier and a little more adventurous than she'd imagined.

Just then, Lizzie heard a tiny bark over the frosty wind. It sounded close by. That bark was followed by another one. Lizzie was sure they were from the same dog. The barks did not sound like a happy dog playing in the snow. They were sharp and loud, like the dog was in trouble.

Lizzie forced herself to move more quickly, tugging her boots out of the deep snow. The park's soccer field looked like a sparkling white ocean, with waves of snowdrifts reaching all across the meadow.

The barks came closer and closer together. To get to Mariko's house, Lizzie needed to go left—but the barks were coming from the right. Lizzie hesitated. She had told her parents she would go straight to her friend's house, but she couldn't ignore a dog in trouble. She was sure they would understand.

Lizzie took a deep breath and trudged toward the barks. For a while, she could only see white. Then a black dot appeared, bouncing up and down through the snow. Lizzie squinted through the snowflakes and realized that the black spot was a nose! Soon, she saw eyes and a pink tongue, too. It was a puppy, with fur so white that it blended in with the snow.

Lizzie's heart swelled as she pushed even faster toward the puppy. When they reached each other, he jumped up and put his paws on her legs. He pricked his oversized triangular ears and looked up at her with sparkling brown eyes as he yipped in excitement.

Who are you? Can you help? Someone needs you. Quick! I can take you there right away!

"Hello," Lizzie said, kneeling next to the excited puppy. She was tempted to take off her gloves so she could bury her hands in his thick white fur. The puppy was gorgeous, from the tip of his fluffy tail to the tip of his shiny black nose. "Wow. A white German shepherd," she breathed. "I've seen pictures of them, but never been near one in real life. You're beautiful!" Lizzie nuzzled the puppy's neck, breathing in his delicious puppy smell. Why were puppies so—so perfect? Lizzie's family had fostered dozens of puppies who needed help, keeping each one just long enough to find it the right forever home—but she never got tired of how special each and every puppy truly was.

The puppy wriggled and yipped again, and Lizzie snapped back to attention. "What are you doing out here all alone? It's pretty cold, little guy." Lizzie reached around the dog's neck and found a red collar. She felt for a license or name tag, but her hands were clumsy inside the padded gloves. "Spirit," she said when she finally found the tag. There was a phone number, too. "It's nice to meet you, Spirit. I wonder if I should call this number and get you home. Do you live around here?" The puppy barked three times and then took a few steps in the other direction.

Lizzie stood back up and looked all around. She thought about what she should do. She could take the puppy to Mariko's house and call from there, but the puppy seemed to want her to go the other way.

Spirit barked once, spun around, and darted off. Lizzie didn't think twice. She followed his tracks through the snow. Even though he was only a puppy, Spirit seemed to have a definite plan. She had to find out what it was.

CHAPTER TWO

Lizzie pushed through the snow, keeping the white puppy in view. Every once in a while, the puppy stopped floundering through the drifts to look back at her. Lizzie could tell he was checking up on her, making sure she was still following him. He was one smart pup!

"I'm coming," Lizzie said, panting. She could see that Spirit was stepping in older tracks through the crusty snow. It looked as if the puppy was following his own path back to where he had started.

Spirit stopped and tilted his head. He stood completely still, ears pricked and nose lifted.

Lizzie stopped, too. As soon as she did, she heard someone calling. The voice was low, but Lizzie was pretty sure the person was yelling for Spirit.

Instead of bounding off, the puppy looked back at Lizzie. He gave two more sharp barks.

Hurry! We're almost there! They need help. We need help. My boy is hurt. Please hurry!

Even though he was very young—Lizzie guessed he was about five months old—Spirit seemed sure that Lizzie would follow him. He had the same confidence she'd seen in other German shepherds, like Champ, another puppy her family had fostered.

Lizzie was also confident—confident that she was close to the far side of the park. That meant there was a road nearby. She listened for a moment. This time, she heard two voices, one high and one low. Spirit heard them, too. He looked back at her again.

"What is it?" Lizzie asked the puppy. She bent over with her hands on her knees, trying to catch her breath. "What is it, boy?" After a moment, she started walking again. As she plodded up to the puppy's side, she saw a car—a car that had slid off the icy road and slammed into a tree. The front end was smashed. Lizzie could see the tracks where the wheels had spun out on the icy snow. She felt a chill go up her back, and she began to move more quickly. Was everyone okay?

A man stood next to the car. The back door was open, and he was leaning in. Lizzie could just make out the figure of a boy about Charles's age in the backseat. Lizzie watched as the man talked to the boy and squeezed his hand.

Spirit took off toward them, with Lizzie close behind him. Just as the puppy was about to reach the car, an ambulance came around the corner with its red lights flashing. It came to a stop in the street. Two people in matching blue coats jumped out and ran over to the car.

Lizzie watched the rush of activity. Since her dad was a firefighter, she was used to being around emergency vehicles. In fact, she recognized Meg, one of the EMTs. EMTs—emergency medical technicians—were the people who helped figure out what kind of injuries a person might have, and whether they needed to be taken to the hospital.

Since she had heard two voices yelling, Lizzie was pretty sure that the boy in the backseat was still conscious, but she also could see that he wasn't moving. One of the EMTs returned to the ambulance and came back with a stretcher.

With all the commotion around the car, the puppy could not get very close. He seemed to understand that he needed to stay out of the way and let the people do their jobs. But he watched everything that was happening very closely. Lizzie walked toward Spirit. The puppy was whining. He stood up and then sat back down.

"Is that your family?" Lizzie asked. Spirit looked up at her with his kind, dark eyes.

My people! I'm worried about them.

"Don't worry," Lizzie told him. "Everything will be okay. These folks know how to help."

Spirit's reaction reminded Lizzie again of Champ, who always seemed to know when something, or someone, needed help. Lizzie wondered if maybe Spirit had the same instinct. That would explain why the puppy had come all the way through the snow to find her.

After a while, the man stepped away from the

car and glanced around. "Spirit!" he called. When his eyes fell on the puppy, he looked relieved. The man leaned over. "Come on, Spirit, here, boy!"

Spirit ran over and nearly jumped into the man's arms. The man scooped him up and ruffled his fur. Then he carried the puppy over to the car.

Lizzie stepped a little closer. Even though she couldn't hear what they were saying, she could hear the excited way the boy inside the car talked to Spirit. Their visit was cut short when the EMTs started to move the boy out of the backseat and onto the stretcher.

The man backed away and put the puppy down. He looked around, as if he was waking from a dream. Lizzie realized he must still be in shock from the accident. She walked toward him and introduced herself.

"Your puppy found me in the park," she explained. "It's like he was looking for help."

The man nodded, still looking dazed. "Spirit ran off just after we crashed. I'm Hank. Hank Leckner. That's my son, Eli. I—I think his leg is broken. Thank goodness that was the worst that happened."

"Is there anything I can do to help?" Lizzie asked.

Mr. Leckner paused. "Do you live around here?"

Lizzie explained that she lived on the other side of the park. "I was on my way to visit my friend Mariko. Mariko Miyano."

The man's face brightened. "The Miyanos live just a couple of houses from us," he said. "Maybe you can help. I need to get Spirit back to our house, since I'm going to ride with Eli in the ambulance."

Meg turned around and smiled. "Mr. Leckner, I know this young lady," she said as she latched a buckle on the stretcher. "You can definitely trust Lizzie with your puppy. She's very reliable, and she knows everything there is to know about dogs."

"Spirit," Eli called, reaching out his arms to the puppy. Spirit whined in answer and put a paw on the stretcher, but Mr. Leckner held out a hand to calm him.

"Eli, buddy," Mr. Leckner said. "You can't hold Spirit right now. We need to get you to the hospital."

As Meg and the other EMT carried the stretcher to the ambulance, Mr. Leckner talked to Lizzie. "I would really appreciate it if you could take Spirit and my car keys to my wife. Mariko knows which house is ours. It looks like I need to get in the ambulance with Eli right now." He nodded at the EMTs as they rolled the stretcher into the back of the emergency vehicle.

"Sure," Lizzie said. "I'd be happy to help."

She heard Eli call out for Spirit again. He sounded so sad. Spirit barked twice, and Mr. Leckner gave him a pat. "You listen to Lizzie, boy. Okay? Be a good puppy," he said. He picked Spirit up and carefully placed the puppy into Lizzie's arms.

"I'm sure he will," Lizzie replied, giving Spirit a squeeze. "After all, it was his plan to get me in the first place!"

Mr. Leckner smiled. "That's true," he said. "Thank you, Lizzie." He rushed off to climb into the ambulance with his son.

Spirit and Lizzie watched as the ambulance took off, red lights flashing. Spirit whimpered softly. Lizzie could already tell that this was one sweet, loyal puppy. She hated to see him separated from Eli. Whenever Lizzie was sick, she always felt better if Buddy was with her.

But right now, Lizzie couldn't think about Buddy. She needed to focus. She had someone else's antsy puppy to deal with, another family's car keys in her coat pocket, and a lot to explain to her friend Mariko.

CHAPTER THREE

Lizzie tried to soothe the little white pup. "Everything will be okay," she said. She stroked his back as she walked toward Mariko's house, but the puppy was not calm. He kept fidgeting, squirming around, and trying to get free.

"What's the matter, boy?" Lizzie asked. "If you stick with me, I'll get you home soon." Now that she could walk on the partially cleared sidewalks, she could make better time. But Spirit kept whining and shifting in her arms.

They were only a block or so from Mariko's by then. "All right. I'll put you down if you promise to be good and stay with me," Lizzie said, trying to sound firm. She hated to let a puppy walk without a leash on, but Spirit seemed so mature. Plus, it wouldn't be easy for him to run far with all this snow. "Do you promise?" Spirit stopped squirming. He replied with a single, short bark.

I can be good!

"It's a deal," Lizzie said, bending down to place Spirit on the icy sidewalk. "Let's go."

The puppy stayed dutifully by Lizzie's side as she made her way to Mariko's house. Lizzie knew that Mariko's dad was extremely allergic to dogs — and cats, and guinea pigs, and probably even fish. Lizzie came up with a simple plan. She would tell Mariko what happened, and then they'd go straight to Spirit's house together. They could hand over the car keys and the puppy, and then they'd go back to Mariko's to make the candy.

When Lizzie rang the Miyanos' doorbell, Spirit sat down next to her. Lizzie looked at him. She admired his feathered tail, the one tiny pink spot on his pointed black nose, and his dark, thoughtful eyes.

"Lizzie!" Mariko said as she opened the door. She stared down at Spirit. "Hey, isn't that one of the Leckners' puppies? What's he doing here with you?"

Mariko's mom, Mrs. Miyano, appeared behind her a moment later. "Oh, that's Spirit. I thought he was going out to live at Crowners' Apple Orchard with his sister Sassy."

"I don't know anything about Sassy or the orchard," Lizzie said. "I just know that Mr. Leckner's car slid off the road down the street and Eli had to go to the hospital."

"What?" Mrs. Miyano said. "What happened?"

Lizzie told as much as she knew, and Mrs. Miyano and Mariko peppered her with questions.

"Goodness," Mrs. Miyano finally said. "As if that family doesn't have enough on their plate just now."

"Their plate?" Lizzie frowned.

"Mrs. Leckner is, like, eight months pregnant," Mariko said, holding her hands way out in front of her stomach. "So they were in a hurry to find homes for all their dog's puppies."

"It was such a cute litter," Mrs. Miyano added. "Six little white balls of fluff. We were visiting every day for a while, and we got to know them all." She sighed, then leaned over and put both hands behind Spirit's ears, giving him a good scratch. Then she stood up. "You should take Spirit to the Leckners' house right away. One more minute on our doorstep and Mariko's dad will be sneezing for hours when he comes home."

Mariko went back inside to get ready. Lizzie thought it really was too bad that Mr. Miyano was allergic. Mariko and her mom both loved dogs so much.

Mariko appeared again in a long, puffy lavender-colored coat and lace-up snow boots with a fuzzy lining. "Let's go," she said, pointing the way.

The two girls and the puppy set off. "That's it, right there," Mariko said after they'd passed a couple of houses. She pointed to a gray, two-story house with a wreath on the door. Spirit took off at once. With great strides, he bounced up onto the porch and stood at the door, his tail wagging in a swirling motion.

Here we are! This is my house! My people are inside. And my mom. I'm happy to be home.

Lizzie and Mariko rushed to catch up. Mariko knocked. "I think their doorbell is broken," she said. "At least it was the last time we visited the puppies." She took off her purple glove and knocked again, harder this time.

In a few moments, Mrs. Leckner opened the door. She smiled at Mariko. Then confusion clouded her face. "What's Spirit doing here?" she asked. She stood in the narrow opening, so Spirit could not nudge his way inside.

"Mrs. Leckner," Mariko began carefully, as if she didn't want to shock her, "this is my friend Lizzie. She, um, saw Mr. Leckner down the street, and he gave her his car keys and asked her to bring Spirit here."

Lizzie reached into her pocket and held the keys out. Lizzie noticed Mrs. Leckner's hands shaking a little as she took them.

"Do you know what happened?" she asked. "Is Eli okay? I just got a jumble of texts from my husband, and I wasn't sure what to do." As she spoke, her hand moved to her very round belly, and she rested it there.

"They slid off the road. Eli might have broken his leg, but he seems fine otherwise. He was being very brave. He was calling for Spirit as they put him on the stretcher," Lizzie explained.

"That boy has a one-track mind," Mrs. Leckner said, shaking her head.

"Mom!" a voice called from inside the house. "Dad just texted again. He said the tow truck is on its way. He said we should take the keys and meet them at the car."

Mrs. Leckner raised her hand to her forehead and stared at the ground. "Nora, you're going to have to come with me," she called back. "I don't want to lose my balance on all this ice." She sighed and looked up again. "But what about Spirit? I thought my husband was taking him to Crowners'

Apple Orchard. They already took his sister Sassy and they'd agreed to take him, too." She reached for a coat hanging on a hook by the door. "I thought I'd seen the last of our crazy puppy days. And now this! I just can't have him here."

"Well, we can't take Spirit because of my dad's allergies, but Lizzie's family is kind of famous for fostering puppies," Mariko said. She put a hand on Lizzie's shoulder and smiled. "I'll bet they can take Spirit, at least for now."

"Oh, that's a great idea, Mariko. Lizzie, our whole family would be so grateful." Mrs. Leckner smiled at Lizzie as she slung her handbag over her shoulder. "Spirit is a super sweet puppy who definitely deserves a good home," she added. She tried to button her coat around her belly, but only the top two buttons would close. "Nora! We have to go!"

Lizzie opened her mouth, then closed it. What was there to say? Of course she had to help Spirit, but she knew she wasn't supposed to take on a new foster puppy without her parents' permission. Before Lizzie could explain the situation, Mrs. Leckner and Nora had pushed past them. Eli's sister looked like she was in middle school; she was almost as tall as her mom and strong enough to help her down the porch stairs.

Spirit started running circles around their legs and yipping excitedly. "It's good to see you, too, Spirit!" Nora said.

"I'm sure Lizzie and her family will take good care of you," Mrs. Leckner said, stooping down with a sigh to pet the puppy's head. And then she and Nora were off.

Lizzie picked Spirit up before he could bolt after them. They watched together as the puppy's first family walked away.

CHAPTER FOUR

Lizzie carried Spirit back to Mariko's house, where Mrs. Miyano met them on the porch with steaming mugs of hot chocolate. "I feel terrible that I can't invite you and Spirit in," said Mrs. Miyano.

"That's okay," said Lizzie. "Spirit and I should be on our way, anyway. But could I use your phone to call my mom? I should at least give her a little warning that I'm bringing home a new foster puppy."

Soon, Lizzie was ready to set off again. She had found a leash at the bottom of her backpack, and she snapped it onto Spirit's collar as she said good-bye to her friend. "Good thing Mom was understanding. I guess she's not surprised anymore when a puppy falls into our laps. Anyway, I'm sorry we can't make the candy today," Lizzie said to Mariko.

"Are you kidding?" Mariko asked between sips from her steaming mug. "You get to foster an awesome puppy. What's better than that?"

Lizzie gave Spirit a scratch between the ears. "You ready, boy?" she asked. Spirit trotted off the porch next to Lizzie, but he seemed to lose his lively energy as they crossed the park, following the trail Lizzie had made on the way over. The puppy kept slowing down to glance back the way they'd come, but Lizzie encouraged him to keep going.

By the time they reached the other side of the park, Spirit was almost dragging. His eagerness was gone, and he seemed like a completely different puppy.

The whole family was there to greet Lizzie and the new puppy when they finally made it back home. "Aww, he's lovely," Mom said, kneeling down to give Spirit a gentle scratch. The Bean approached him carefully, the way he'd been taught with new puppies, then gave Spirit a mighty hug. Spirit didn't seem to mind one bit. He just turned his head to give the Bean's hair a good sniff. Charles petted Spirit's ears while Dad examined his big, chunky feet. Through it all Spirit was calm—*almost too calm*, Lizzie thought. He didn't seem all that excited about meeting his new foster family.

"Is Buddy outside?" Lizzie asked. The family liked to introduce Buddy to new foster dogs in the backyard, where there was more space to run and play and get to know each other. Buddy was such a friendly, easygoing puppy that they rarely had problems. As soon as Lizzie opened the door,

Spirit scrambled down the snowy stairs and ran right up to Buddy. Buddy sniffed the fluffy white pup all over and then ran off, inviting Spirit to play.

Watching Spirit leap after Buddy, Lizzie felt a little better. The new puppy seemed happy and confident again. He ran in circles around Buddy. It was funny how Spirit's black nose and dangling pink tongue really stood out in the snow.

While she watched the two puppies romp, Lizzie told her family everything she had learned about Spirit and the Leckners. Mariko had explained that Eli was a year younger than Charles, and Nora was in her first year at the nearby middle school. When Mom found out that Mrs. Leckner was eight months pregnant, she was very understanding. "Having two kids and six puppies is enough work even when you aren't pregnant!" she said.

Lizzie had also heard from Mariko and her mom that the Leckners had found homes for all the other puppies even before Mitzy, the mother dog, had the litter. "That must have taken a lot of planning," Dad said, sounding impressed. Lizzie had to agree. She knew how much work it took to find the right home for just one puppy.

Mariko knew where every other puppy had ended up, but she had no idea why Spirit had not stayed at the apple orchard with his sister.

Now, Lizzie looked out the window again. Spirit and Buddy seemed to be getting along well. Spirit bowed down with his front paws stretched out and barked happily. Buddy dashed clear across the snowy yard and tackled Spirit with all his might. Spirit rolled over, his mouth open wide as if he were laughing.

"They're just a couple of goofballs," Mom said, gazing out the kitchen window.

Now Lizzie understood why Mrs. Leckner had thought the puppies were so wild. Spirit was like a completely different dog when he was at play! Watching Spirit with Buddy, Lizzie thought that Spirit might like a home that had another dog. He was so much happier now than he had been when they were walking across the park.

"Buddy! Spirit!" Lizzie went to the door to call the dogs in. It was so cold outside, and Spirit had spent most of his day in the snow. That was a lot for such a young puppy, even if he did seem to be having fun. Spirit and Buddy tried to climb the slick steps, side by side. Lizzie giggled. They kept knocking into each other, their tails whipping around in the air. "Come on, guys," Lizzie said. "Let me get your paws." The puppies waited patiently as Lizzie wiped the snow and ice chunks from their feet with an old towel. Buddy even licked her face as a thank-you.

When Lizzie was done, Buddy trotted over to where Charles was reading in the living room. Buddy nosed his way onto the beanbag chair and curled up in Charles's lap. Charles started to scratch Buddy's neck, and Buddy laid his head on Charles's chest.

Seeing them, Lizzie felt the urge to curl up with a book, too. It was that kind of day. But first, she wanted to get the new puppy settled in his temporary home. "Hey, Spirit," she said, turning to the sweet white pup. "Are you hungry? Want some food?" Spirit didn't seem that interested, but Lizzie got out the extra food and water bowls, just to be sure. After she had filled them both, she set them down next to Buddy's empty dishes. "Here you go, boy. You've had a busy day. You must be starving."

But Spirit was still sitting in the same spot

where she had left him, staring into the living room. He was watching Charles and Buddy.

Where am I? This isn't my place. Those aren't my food bowls. Where are all my brothers and sisters? And my mom?

Lizzie decided to call the owners of Crowners' Apple Orchard and find out why they hadn't taken Spirit. She knew the orchard well. In the summer, the owners ran a farm stand by the road. They sold the best apple-cider doughnuts, fresh out of the fryer. They sold good apples, too. If Dad was making an apple pie, he insisted on getting the tart green apples from Crowners'.

The phone rang a few times before someone picked up. When they did, Lizzie could hear a puppy's friendly yips on the other end. "Hello?"

a woman said. Lizzie could picture Mrs. Crowner's kind face with her tiny glasses and pale blue eyes.

"Hello? Mrs. Crowner?" Lizzie began. "My name is Lizzie Peterson. I'm helping the Leckner family with one of their puppies, Spirit."

"Oh, yes," Mrs. Crowner said. "We met Spirit this morning. We adopted his sister Sassy."

"Yes, Mrs. Leckner told me that," Lizzie replied, trying to think of what to say next. She glanced at Spirit, who was lying down in the same spot by the door, his eyes big and his ears pricked as he watched Buddy and Charles cuddle. Lizzie quickly told Mrs. Crowner about all the events of the day. "So now," she finished, "Spirit is here with us. He's safe and sound, but he seems to really be missing his littermates."

"Oh, Lizzie," Mrs. Crowner said. "We had planned to take both puppies, but those two were just too rambunctious together. They were cute and loud and happy, and we could see right away that two puppies would be too much for Mr. Crowner and me to keep track of. My sister told me that brother and sister puppies can often be a real handful—they enjoy each other so much that they really don't pay attention to their people. That's what made us rethink our decision."

"But—" Lizzie began, then stopped. She knew the Crowners would take two puppies if they could. What was the point of persuading them to take on more than they could handle? Lizzie thanked the older woman and hung up the phone.

She knelt down next to Spirit and stroked his silky ears, which still felt chilly from his time outside. "You're a sweet guy, Spirit. We'll find you a good home. I promise." The puppy looked up at her with glistening eyes, let out a long sigh, and laid his head between his paws.

CHAPTER FIVE

At school the next day, Lizzie kept thinking about Spirit. She knew he was safe at home. He had food and water, and Buddy to play with if he was feeling lonely, but Lizzie was still worried. The puppy seemed to be having a hard time settling in. Lizzie needed to figure out what kind of home would be best for him.

At lunch, Mariko found Lizzie right away. "Hey, how's Spirit?" she asked, sitting down across from Lizzie and Maria. "Want some edamame?" she asked, holding out a metal dish of green beans that she ate straight from the pod.

Lizzie took a few beans. She shook her head as she popped them into her mouth. "I'm not sure about Spirit," she said. "He was so happy playing with Buddy, but then he came inside and just sort of moped around. I couldn't get him to eat or play with any of Buddy's toys. He'd sniff them and then look away. It was really sad."

"What about that new toy?" Maria asked, tucking her shiny dark hair behind her ear. "The orange one that you can put the treats in, and then throw it across the room?" Maria had been with Lizzie when she had used her dog-walking money to buy that toy for Buddy.

"Nothing," Lizzie answered. "I even put two different flavors of treats in there, just in case Spirit had a favorite. But he barely sniffed it."

"Maybe he was just tired," Maria suggested. Maria had a strong instinct for animals.

"Sometimes, after a long day of errands and stuff, Simba just needs to sleep." Simba, a big yellow Lab, was Maria's mom's guide dog.

"That makes sense," Lizzie said. "Simba would be tired after a full day of work." She peeled an orange, thinking about what Maria said. "Spirit is still a puppy, and yesterday must have been exhausting for him. Maybe he'll feel better today."

"I'm going to take Eli's homework to him after school," Mariko said. "He did break his leg, and he has a big cast on it. He'll be home for a while. He can't use crutches or a wheelchair in all this snow and ice. You guys want to come with me?"

"Sorry, I have a riding lesson," Maria said. "My show is next week."

"I can come," Lizzie said. "I'll meet you outside your room after the bell." She was glad that she had asked the other partners in her dog-walking business to cover their customers until she found a home for Spirit. That meant she was free after school. It would be fun to walk home with Mariko, and it would also give Lizzie one more chance to talk to the Leckners. Even if they didn't want Spirit, they might know someone who would. Maybe they had a waiting list for their puppies.

It seemed like a lot had happened since the last time Lizzie had stepped foot on the Leckners' porch. This time, when Mrs. Leckner answered, she looked much more relaxed. "Thanks so much for bringing Eli's homework," she said, taking the cloth bag from Mariko. "I really appreciate it." She paused for a moment and looked over her shoulder. "Hey, Eli!" she called. "You'll be happy to know that Mariko brought your homework, so you won't have to play video games all afternoon!"

Lizzie thought she heard a groan from deep inside the house.

Mrs. Leckner turned back to the girls. "I have a big project for work that is due this week. It's my last one before the baby, and I'm having a hard time getting it done with Eli always asking for a snack or for something off his shelf." She smiled. "Poor guy. He's pretty bored. Hopefully this homework will keep him busy."

Just then, a beautiful white German shepherd nosed her way out the door and onto the porch with Lizzie and Mariko. Lizzie knew right away that she must be Spirit's mother. She and Spirit had the same kind, intelligent expression.

"Mitzy," Mrs. Leckner said with a laugh, "are you bored, too? Do you need some attention, girl?"

Before Mrs. Leckner could call the dog back in, Lizzie and Mariko knelt down to give her a proper greeting.

"Hi there, Mitzy," Mariko said, stroking the dog's back.

Mitzy sniffed Lizzie all over. Her nose made a snuffly sound as it rubbed up against Lizzie's puffy coat. Then she looked up at Lizzie, tilting her head to one side.

"You smell Spirit, don't you?" Lizzie asked. She laughed out loud when Mitzy gave her a warm, wet lick. Dog licks always made Lizzie happy. "Hi, Mitzy," she said softly. "It's really nice to meet you, too."

"Okay, Mitzy, that's enough," Mrs. Leckner said, trying to pull the dog away. "Nora! Could you come get the dog? She's attacking our guests with slobber."

"Aw, that's so sweet." Nora, Eli's big sister, had joined her mom at the door. "I'll bet she can smell Spirit on Lizzie. Mitzy probably really misses her puppies."

Mrs. Leckner laughed again. "She misses them more than I do, I think."

"But they were adorable," Nora said. She smiled at Lizzie as she grabbed Mitzy's collar.

"True," Mrs. Leckner admitted. "They were adorable—to a point. They were also wild little tornadoes. It's nice to have a little quiet in the house."

"Before the baby comes," Nora said, guiding Mitzy back inside.

"Before the baby comes," Mrs. Leckner repeated.

"How's Spirit doing?" Nora asked Lizzie.

Lizzie hesitated. "He's fine," she said. "But I think he misses all of you."

Nora nodded. "We miss him, too." She petted Mitzy. "Good thing we still have one dog to keep us company."

Lizzie asked whether they'd had a waiting list for the puppies.

Mrs. Leckner shook her head. "We stopped

asking around after we thought we'd found them all homes," she explained.

Lizzie had a much better feeling about the Leckners after her and Mariko's visit that day. She could tell how much they loved Mitzy. She could also tell that they had enjoyed Mitzy's puppies—but she understood why they'd given them away. Too bad they didn't have any good ideas about another nice family who was ready to adopt a sweet, energetic puppy of their own.

CHAPTER SIX

"Buddy! Spirit!" Lizzie called for the puppies as soon as she arrived home, but neither of them came to the door to welcome her. Lizzie thought that was strange. Buddy almost always raced into the front hallway, his nails clacking against the wood floor.

"We're in here!" Mom called from the kitchen. Now Lizzie could guess why Buddy hadn't run to see her. If someone was cooking, he always liked to hang out in the kitchen in case any food scraps needed vacuuming up.

"What are you making?" Lizzie asked as she

hung up her coat and started to unload her backpack.

"Nola!" the Bean told her. That was his word for "granola."

Lizzie felt her stomach grumble. It had been a long walk across the park, even though the weather was warmer today and the snow had packed down. She went into the kitchen. Sure enough, she found Buddy staring longingly up at the counter, where all the ingredients for granola were spread out. The Bean was snacking on dried cranberries. Mom's hands were sticky with a paste of butter, oats, and brown sugar.

"How was your day?" Mom asked.

"Fine, I guess," Lizzie said. "How was Spirit while I was gone?"

Mom paused. "Fine, I guess."

"What does that mean?" Lizzie asked.

"Well, to be honest he was kind of mopey," Mom said.

"Where is he now?" Lizzie leaned over to give Buddy a pat. Buddy wagged his tail and glanced at Lizzie, then went back to staring at the action on the kitchen counter, licking his chops.

"I think he's in the living room," Mom said.

Lizzie left the kitchen to track down the white puppy. "Hey, Spirit," she said when she found him sleeping by the beanbag chair. The puppy blinked a few times, but he didn't raise his head. "Do you want to go out? You can play with Buddy." Spirit took a deep breath and let out a long sigh, head still on his paws. "Come on." Lizzie patted her leg. "Time to go out."

Spirit stood up and plodded after Lizzie.

"Time to go out!" Lizzie said again, loud enough for Buddy to hear. As soon as Spirit heard the jingle of Buddy's collar, he perked up. He broke into a trot and stayed right on Lizzie's heels, almost tripping her.

Is it time to play? With the other dog? Hooray! I love to play. Are we going outside? That's even better! I can't wait!

Buddy met them at the door, and both puppies barked in excitement. The moment Lizzie let them out, they began to wrestle and chase. Spirit could not have been happier!

Lizzie smiled as she watched them from inside, but she was still concerned about Spirit. He was so full of energy and joy when he was outside playing with another dog. Why was he so quiet and mopey inside? It didn't make any sense.

"Hey," Charles said, coming into the kitchen. "Where's Buddy?"

"He's in the yard with Spirit," Lizzie said without turning around.

Charles came over to watch out the window. He giggled when Spirit began to roll on his back in the snow, sliding down one of the drifts. Buddy reared up on his hind legs and then dropped onto Spirit, nipping at the white puppy's tail.

"German shepherds are supposed to be smart, right?" Charles said. "So maybe you should find out if he could be a service dog or police dog. Or he could do search and rescue. He did track you down all the way across the park, right?"

Lizzie was surprised she hadn't thought of that. She had been so focused on how much Spirit liked to play with Buddy that she had only thought of him as a family dog—a family dog who needed another dog in the family.

Still, Charles was right. Spirit had shown signs

that he might have a natural instinct for helping, just like Champ. He had known Eli was in trouble and had tried to seek out help. Plus, Spirit had stayed close to Eli and Mr. Leckner while the EMTs were busy, but had also seemed to know he should keep out of the way. Those were all good instincts for a working dog.

"That's a great idea, Charles," Lizzie said. "Spirit is super intelligent, and he has a really willing and helpful personality." Lizzie looked out at Buddy and Spirit in the snow. She could just picture Spirit wearing one of those colored vests that indicated the dog was at work. A bright blue or orange vest would look amazing against his pure white coat.

Since the two puppies were still enjoying themselves, Lizzie went upstairs to the computer to research some organizations she could call. She knew that training programs took several months, and the programs were very picky; they took only the best dogs, the ones who could prove they were intelligent, brave, and calm. Lizzie believed Spirit could pass any of their tests. Couldn't he?

CHAPTER SEVEN

By the middle of the week, Lizzie had a routine. She let Spirit and Buddy outside as soon as she got home. That way, they had plenty of time to play before it got cold and dark. Spirit loved to play in the yard with Buddy, but he still seemed bored and lonely when he was in the house.

Days had passed since Lizzie had called the police department, the service-dog training center, and the Search and Rescue Dog Association. She had left messages everywhere. Now she was waiting to hear back. She was sure that Spirit was the kind of dog who needed a job, who wanted to work and feel useful. She crossed her fingers and hoped that one of the organizations had a spot open for the smart white pup.

On Wednesday, after she let the puppies outside, Lizzie started to make a snack. She took one of Mom's granola bars from the tin and poured a glass of milk. Charles walked in as she was putting the milk back in the refrigerator.

Her brother went straight to the back door and opened it. "Buddy! Spirit!" he called.

"What are you doing?" Lizzie asked. "I just put them out."

"I have to do my reading homework," he said. "I need Buddy."

Lizzie rolled her eyes and left the kitchen in search of Mom. She was upstairs, working at her desk. "Mom! Charles is calling the dogs, but I *just* put them out."

Mom looked up and shook her head. "I know Spirit likes to play," she said, "but you know how Buddy and Charles love to read together."

Lizzie sighed. By the time she got back to the kitchen, Charles and Buddy were already in the other room. Spirit walked over to his bowl and gulped some water. "Hi, Spirit," Lizzie said, patting her leg. The puppy ignored her, heading for the living room instead. Lizzie followed him.

Charles was nestled in the beanbag chair with Buddy. They looked cozy. Spirit gazed at them with his deep brown eyes. He began to whimper.

Is it snuggle time? I want to snuggle. Where is my boy?

"What is it, Spirit?" Lizzie asked, stroking the puppy's back. "Do you want to sit and read? We can do that." Lizzie grabbed a book and sat down on the floor next to the puppy, leaning against the couch. Spirit got down on his haunches, but he didn't cuddle with Lizzie. He stared at Charles and Buddy, whining quietly. Lizzie read out loud. She scratched Spirit behind the ears. She tried to get him to climb into her lap. No matter what Lizzie did, she could not distract him from the other two, reading cozily in the chair.

When the weekend came, not much had changed. Spirit was full of energy whenever he was outside with Buddy, but he was the opposite as soon as he came into the house. Lizzie didn't want to leave him for a whole day. Still, she wanted to see Mariko. They had a project to finish. "Can Mariko come over?" she asked Mom. "We still want to make that maple syrup candy."

"That sounds delicious," Mom said, "but also

messy. Promise me you'll clean up the kitchen when you're done?"

Lizzie agreed.

Dad, Charles, and Buddy left after breakfast to run errands. Mariko arrived soon after that.

"How's Spirit?" she asked while taking off her fancy snow boots.

"He's okay," Lizzie said. "I'm still waiting to hear from all the organizations I called." Hearing his name, Spirit appeared in the front hallway. He seemed to perk up when he saw Mariko.

"Hey, Spirit," she said, approaching him with her hand stretched out. "Remember me? How are you, boy?" Mariko sat down in the middle of the floor and pulled the puppy into her lap for a hug.

"He really likes you," Lizzie said, noting how content Spirit looked. The puppy rubbed his head against Mariko's sweater and looked up at her with those deep brown eyes.

I remember you from my house. You're so nice. You are good at snuggling, too.

"And I really like him," Mariko said. "I also really like maple syrup candy. I brought all the stuff. Want to get started?"

Mariko had gone on a camping trip where her family took a "sugaring hike" and had learned all about how to make maple syrup. As the two girls pulled out pans and measuring cups, Mariko told Lizzie all about it.

"Most people think of maple syrup as being something that says 'winter,'" Mariko began. "It has a warm, sweet taste that seems nice and cozy, but the truth is that sap doesn't start flowing in the maple trees until the first signs of spring." Mariko was good at talking while she worked. Lizzie thought that she sounded just like a tour guide. Mariko was already busy stirring the maple syrup on the stovetop. "When the temperature gets above freezing, the sap moves through the trees again. That's when people put the taps into the tree trunks, so the sap will drip out."

"Yum," Lizzie said, thinking about how cool it was that maple syrup came straight from nature.

"Double yum," said Mom, who had just come into the kitchen. She sniffed the fragrant steam coming off the pan. "Is it done?"

Mariko held up the hand with the candy thermometer in it. "Not quite yet," she said. "Anyway, sap is, like, ninety-eight percent water. It doesn't taste like much of anything. The syrup makers have to boil it down for hours and hours until most of the water evaporates. That's when it becomes syrup. It takes forty gallons of sap to make one gallon of syrup!"

Mom stood with the refrigerator door open, listening. "That's interesting. I don't think I ever knew that," she said.

Mariko nodded. "They do it in a little cabin called a 'sugar shack.'"

It was Lizzie's turn to stir now, and her arm was already tired. Mariko explained that they didn't want the syrup to stick to the bottom of the pan, or else it would burn. Eventually, the maple syrup started to boil.

"Once the thermometer reads two hundred forty degrees, we let it cool," Mariko advised. "Then we pour it into molds, and then we let it cool more."

Lizzie was used to baking with Mom, but working on the stovetop with hot liquids was new. Mom never would have let Lizzie pour boiling hot candy, but Mariko seemed like a pro. Mariko's mom had given Mariko permission to let her use the stove at Lizzie's house.

"The good news is that it's still cold outside," Mariko said as she lifted the pan to pour the frothy syrup. Mom steadied the tray of heart-shaped molds. "So we can let the candy set in a deep bank of snow. That's the old-fashioned way to do it. It needs to get pretty cold."

"That is good news," Lizzie agreed as they carried the mold outside. "Is there also bad news?"

Mariko nodded. "Yeah, that it's still cold outside. That's been rough on Eli. All this snow and ice means he's still stuck inside. I feel awful for him. Nora said he can't play with his basketball team or anything. He usually builds snow forts and goes sledding all winter. He's getting really bummed out." She sighed.

Later, as Lizzie and Mariko carried the cooled

candy back inside, Lizzie had an idea. "Hey, maybe we should take some of our maple syrup candy to the Leckners' house to help him feel better," she said.

Mom came into the kitchen. "I think we should talk before you make any plans to visit Spirit's first family," she said. "We don't want to bother them when they're so overwhelmed."

CHAPTER EIGHT

"It's okay. My mom already talked to the Leckners," Mariko said. "They're expecting us."

She explained that Mrs. Miyano had offered to send over dinner because she knew Mrs. Leckner was trying to finish her project, and take Eli to doctors' appointments, and go to Nora's gymnastics meet. They were one busy family.

Mom was convinced. "As long as you aren't intruding, I suppose it's all right," she said.

"We won't even go inside," Lizzie assured her. Then she paused. "Can I take Spirit?" she asked. "Buddy's been out with Dad and Charles all day, so Spirit could really use the exercise."

Mom said yes, and Lizzie rushed to get the leash. She was relieved. The walk would be so much more fun with Spirit. Plus, she really wanted the Leckners to see him again and remember what a great puppy he was. Maybe she could explain how he was super rowdy only when he was around his siblings.

Spirit's mood improved as they crossed the park. "We're going on a visit," Lizzie said. Spirit began to hold his tail higher as he jogged along next to Lizzie. He even started to tug on the leash as they neared his old house.

Mrs. Miyano met them on the sidewalk. She held a long glass dish with foil on top. It looked like lasagna to Lizzie. Mrs. Miyano also had a cotton bag over her shoulder. Two long, skinny loaves of crusty bread stuck out of the top. She noticed Lizzie admiring them. "There's a salad in there, too," she said.

Lizzie's mouth watered, and she wondered what her family was having for dinner.

"Our candy turned out great," Mariko said. She added the heart-shaped sweets to Mrs. Miyano's bag. She and Lizzie had wrapped them up with a yellow bow at the top. "It's just the right creamy color," she told her mom.

"Good work, you two. Now, let's go," Mrs. Miyano said with an approving nod. She strode toward the Leckners' porch with purpose. She pushed the doorbell and waited.

"It's still broken," Mariko noted. "I guess they really are busy, if they haven't had time to fix it."

As soon as Mrs. Miyano knocked, they heard a bark from the other side of the door.

Spirit barked right back. His tail began to wag in its swishy, circular way. He ran right up to the door, reached out with a paw, and gave it a scratch.

That's my mom. I'm sure of it! I'm so excited to see her again.

"Steady, boy," Lizzie said. She wondered if it had been a bad idea to bring him. What if she got the puppy's hopes up? What if he acted too rowdy?

As soon as the door opened, Mitzy slipped out. Spirit began to yip with joy. Mitzy barked, too. She reached out her nose and gave Spirit's whole face a giant lick. Spirit ran in circles all around her. He even ducked under her belly a few times and popped out on the other side with a playful yip.

"Easy, Spirit," said Lizzie.

But Mr. Leckner didn't seem to mind. "Spirit! It's good to see you again," he said. He crouched down to give the puppy a good pet before he even said hello to Mrs. Miyano and the girls. When he stood back up, he gave the Miyanos and Lizzie a kind smile. "It's good to see all of you, too."

"Hello, Hank," Mrs. Miyano said. "We brought you some dinner. It'll be very easy to heat up when everyone else gets home." She held out the casserole dish with both hands. Once Mr. Leckner had a good hold, she looped the handles of the cloth bag around one of his thumbs.

"This is really too much," he said, looking embarrassed. "We're already so grateful for all you've done. Especially you, Lizzie." He then looked right at her. "It's such a great thing you and your family are doing. We really appreciate that you're going to find the right home for Spirit."

"We're happy to help," Lizzie said. "He really is a special puppy." By now she was on her knees, petting Spirit and Mitzy at the same time.

"Lizzie made a bunch of calls to different places to see if Spirit might be a service or police dog," Mariko said. "Can you imagine if your puppy was

trained to help with search and rescue or something like that?"

"That would be pretty amazing," Mr. Leckner
admitted. He excused himself so he could put the
food on a nearby table. When he came back, he
knelt down again to play with Spirit. "This guy
was one of my favorites in the litter. He was so
cute. He loved to play with his brothers and sisters. They'd get so rowdy!"

"Sometimes sibling puppies are like that,"
Lizzie said. "That's why the Crowners changed
their minds."

Mr. Leckner looked thoughtful. "Sometimes
people do that." He paused, and then added,
"Sometimes people change their minds."

Lizzie held her breath, waiting to hear him say
that he had changed his mind, and that the
Leckners wanted Spirit back. But he was silent.
"What about the families that took the other

puppies?" Lizzie asked hopefully. "Maybe one of them would like a second one. They could keep each other company."

"I wish," Mr. Leckner said. "We've actually already called them all. I took care of that after Eli got back from the hospital and things calmed down a bit. No such luck."

Lizzie tried to hide her disappointment.

"Don't worry, Hank," Mrs. Miyano said. "Things will work out."

"The Petersons will find Spirit the perfect for-ever home," Mariko promised. "They always do."

Lizzie tried to smile. It was nice that her friend had so much faith in her. She looked at Mr. Leckner. She could tell he was trying to be hope-ful, too. As she stood to go, a pile of books on the hall table caught her eye. "Hey, I recognize those books," she said, hoping to change the subject. "Those are my brother's favorites."

Mr. Leckner turned around. "Those are Eli's," he said. "He just rips through those graphic novels, especially when he's stuck in bed all day. Not too much else to do."

"They're pretty good," Lizzie said. "I've read them all, too."

Lizzie needed to tug a little on the leash when it was time to go. Spirit was not ready to leave. Mr. Leckner had to do the same to Mitzy's collar.

"Maybe you could bring Spirit by again," Mr. Leckner said. "For a visit. Before he goes to his forever home."

Lizzie thought she noticed a wistful note in his voice. "Of course," she said. "He'd love that." A tiny hope began to take hold inside her. Maybe Spirit's perfect forever family was his first family.

CHAPTER NINE

The visit to the Leckners' house really stuck with Lizzie. She thought about their family a lot. Of course, she was disappointed that the Leckners' lives were so busy. She wished that they could keep Spirit, but she understood their decision.

She thought that her family and their family had a lot in common. After all, the oldest Leckner kid was a girl. There was a younger brother, and they were expecting a third child, too. Plus, they obviously liked dogs.

She had also been thinking about what Mariko had said about Eli. Lizzie felt bad that he was stuck inside with nothing to do. She decided to go to the library and check out some books he might like. She knew of another graphic novel series, similar to the one Eli and Charles loved so much. She just hoped some of the books were on the library shelf.

Lizzie stopped at the library on her way home from school the next day. She couldn't believe her good luck. The library had all the books in the series in stock. That never happened! Lizzie took it as a good sign, and she checked out the whole series. She couldn't wait to take them to Eli.

Lizzie had always heard that good news came in threes. On her way home, she wondered what other good things might happen. One, she had the whole afternoon free to play with Spirit and Buddy. Two, she had found all the books she had wanted at the library. That left the possibility that one more good thing—number three—was still to come. She crossed her fingers, hoping that one of the organizations had called. Finding out that Spirit had a spot in a training program would be the best news of all!

Lizzie had convinced herself that Spirit would be an excellent working dog. The night before, Spirit had come to the rescue yet again. The Bean had caught his hand in a cabinet door, and it was Spirit who had rushed to find someone who could help. Then, after Mom had come running, Spirit stayed with the Bean until his hand was free. Spirit even licked the Bean's ear to distract him. The Bean thought it was hilarious. He giggled when Spirit's cold, wet nose hit his cheek. He didn't even cry when Mom cleaned out his cut. Mom had said Spirit was "a real lifesaver."

Even after the Bean had calmed down, Spirit stayed by his side. The puppy crawled right into the Bean's bed that night and curled up next to him for his bedtime story. Lizzie had taken a picture on Mom's phone and sent it to the Leckners, along with the story about how Spirit had helped her little brother.

Now, as Lizzie arrived home from the library, she saw Dad in the driveway. He was whacking the sharp end of a shovel against the thick, hard-packed ice. It looked like hard work. Dad stopped to wipe the sweat off his forehead. That was when he noticed Lizzie. He grinned and waved, propping himself on the shovel as she approached. "Hi, Lizzie," he said. "How was your day?"

"Good," Lizzie answered. "Actually, it was pretty great." Lizzie got ready to tell Dad all about her library success, but then she saw the smile drop from his face. "What is it?" she asked.

"Sorry to tell you," Dad said. "But I heard from the police chief. He says he's sorry, but he doesn't have any officers who are looking for a canine partner right now."

Lizzie sighed. The extra books in her backpack suddenly felt really heavy. She shifted it off her shoulders and let it drop to her feet.

"He did mention that they'll have a new class starting in the spring," Dad added. His tone was upbeat, but Lizzie and Dad both knew that spring was too late. Spirit needed his new life to start now. He was ready. He had way too much to offer to have to wait several more months.

"Thanks, Dad," Lizzie said, forcing a smile. She yanked the backpack off the ground and headed for the house. The bag's bottom brushed against the snow as she walked.

"Oh! I think your mom took a message for you earlier," Dad called out just before Lizzie reached the door.

Lizzie felt her heart lift. Maybe the search-and-rescue association or the service-dog program had called to say they had a spot for Spirit.

"Mom! Mom!" Lizzie was calling, even before she'd stepped in the door. She kicked off her boots and left her bag in the entry hallway. "Mom!"

"Goodness, Lizzie," Mom said, appearing in the kitchen doorway with a crumpled dish towel in her hands. "What is it?" The Bean walked up behind Mom and peeked through her legs.

"Dad said you have a message for me?"

Mom nodded. "It's not good news, I'm sorry to say. The search-and-rescue people called to say they have no trainers available for new dogs right now."

Lizzie's face fell. "Ugh." She sighed and kicked at her dropped backpack. "I think I'll take Spirit for a walk." If she couldn't find the sweet puppy a home, at least she could take the books to Eli. At least then she'd feel like she accomplished something. Plus, hadn't Mr. Leckner said he wanted to see Spirit again? Lizzie had a feeling he might be missing the sweet white pup.

"All right," Mom said. "Be home by dinner."

Lizzie found Spirit sleeping by the beanbag chair. She rubbed his head. The short fur on his ears was so, so soft. "Want to go for a walk?"

The puppy opened his eyes, blinked, then jumped up eagerly.

Of course I want to go for a walk—especially if I get to visit my mom again!

CHAPTER TEN

Even with all the books in it, Lizzie's backpack was a lot lighter after she took out her lunch box and her other school stuff. With Spirit bounding at her side, Lizzie already felt much better. He was such a sweet, smart dog. One way or another, she knew she'd find him a great home.

As they came to the edge of the park, Spirit began to tug on the leash. "Easy, boy," said Lizzie. She would need to work on his leash manners.

"Yes, we're going to your old house," Lizzie said, looking down at the puppy. His ears were pointed forward and his eyes were bright. "Please remember to stay calm. Don't get all rowdy."

Lizzie realized that she should have called before she left. What if they weren't home? She could always leave the books inside their screen door if they weren't there. The books would be safe and stay dry. Still, Spirit would be sad if he did not get to visit his mom and his old family. Lizzie would be disappointed, too.

At the sight of the house, Spirit barked and flashed a doggy smile up at Lizzie. "That's right—we're almost there," Lizzie said. Spirit's tail swished and spun in its happy wag as they climbed the porch steps. It made Lizzie laugh. Lizzie started to take off her glove to knock, but she decided to try the doorbell, just in case. When she pressed the round button, a *ding-dong* followed. "They fixed it!" Lizzie said to Spirit.

Mr. Leckner looked surprised when he opened the door. "Hey, everyone," he called over his shoulder, "it's Lizzie and Spirit."

"Hi," Lizzie said. "I was at the library, and I got some books for Eli." She shrugged her backpack off one shoulder and started to unzip it. By the time she glanced up, the entire Leckner family had gathered by the door—even Eli and Mitzy! Lizzie swallowed down a gulp, feeling suddenly shy. "Um, hi, everyone."

Spirit wasn't so shy. He sprang forward to sniff at Mitzy, his tail wagging harder than ever.

It's Mom! Oh, I really missed her! And my boy! I haven't seen him for so long!

Mitzy nuzzled Spirit with her nose and wagged her tail as her puppy darted all around her. Spirit pulled hard on the leash and it slipped out of Lizzie's hand. The library books tumbled from her arms onto the porch.

"Oh, I'm so sorry!" Lizzie said as she grabbed for the leash. This was *not* how she had meant the visit to go. "I didn't mean to cause a commotion," she said. "Spirit, come here, boy. Calm down now." Spirit jogged back to Lizzie at once. He sat down, his tail still wagging across the boards of the porch. Lizzie gave him a pat and started to pick up the fallen books.

"It's good to see you, Lizzie," Mrs. Leckner said. "We were just talking about you."

Nora knelt down to help Lizzie with the books.

"About me?" Lizzie asked.

"Well, and Spirit," Nora said. Hearing his name, Spirit walked over to Nora and stuck his nose right in her face. "Yes," Nora said, ruffling the fur around the puppy's neck. "We *were* talking about you, Spirit, weren't we?"

"We loved getting that picture of Spirit with your little brother last night," Mrs. Leckner said. "It got us thinking."

By then, Spirit had wandered straight into the Leckners' house, but no one seemed to mind. He went up to Eli and put a gentle paw on the armrest of the boy's wheelchair.

"We have family reading time at night, and Spirit was the only puppy who would actually stay still while we sat and read," Mr. Leckner explained. "Your picture reminded us of that."

"He would always curl up with me," Eli added softly, stroking Spirit's back.

Suddenly, Lizzie understood why Spirit had always seemed so sad when he watched Charles and Buddy cuddle together.

"That's sweet," Lizzie said. She had not seen Eli since the day of the accident. He looked pretty happy for someone whose leg was all wrapped in plaster and propped up in front of him like a board. Eli scratched Spirit under the neck, and the puppy lifted his chin up high. Then Eli bent to pull Spirit into a great, big hug. His parents watched and smiled.

"That's one of the reasons I think Spirit would be a great service dog," Lizzie said. "He's very patient and brave. And intelligent. But I haven't heard back from the training center yet. You sometimes have to wait a while for an open spot."

"So you really think Spirit has what it takes?" Mrs. Leckner asked.

"Oh, definitely." Lizzie stood up and handed the stack of books to Mr. Leckner.

Nora stood up, too. Then she turned to look at Lizzie. "What my parents really want to ask is, do you think Spirit would be better as a service dog than a pet? Because ever since you sent that picture, we have all been thinking that we'd love to have him come back to live with us. He could keep Eli company. He could keep Mitzy company. He'd be sort of like a service dog for our whole family."

Lizzie frowned. "Really?" she asked. "I thought you didn't want a hyper, rowdy puppy in the house. Because, you know . . ." She looked at Mrs. Leckner. "You're having a baby."

"I know, I know," Mrs. Leckner said, her hand moving to her belly. "It will be a lot of work, having a puppy and a baby, but I think our family can handle it."

"I promised to help a lot," Eli said. "Even more when my cast comes off."

"And I can make sure Eli does what he says he'll do," added Nora, sounding like a typical older sister.

Lizzie held her breath. Was this really happening?

"Besides," said Mr. Leckner, "Spirit isn't nearly

as rambunctious when he's not with his siblings. He's playful with Mitzy, but he isn't out of control."

"You're right," agreed Mrs. Leckner. "Without his littermates around, he's a lot more mellow."

"You know? I think this is exactly what Spirit has wanted all along— to be back with his mom and his people," said Lizzie. "And, secretly, I did, too!"

"So you think it's a good idea?" asked Mrs. Leckner.

"I think it's a great idea," said Lizzie.

Spirit licked Eli's face in celebration, and Eli gave him another hug.

Lizzie couldn't wait to tell her family and the Miyanos. This was the best news ever. Her wish had come true. Spirit had found the perfect forever home—with his very own family!

PUPPY TIPS

German shepherds are one of the most loyal, trainable dog breeds. They become very attached to their owners and will do anything for the people they love. They can be trained as police dogs, search-and-rescue dogs, or service dogs — but they make wonderful family pets as well. They need plenty of exercise and, as Lizzie noted, they love to have a job to do.

Dear Reader,

I've always thought that white German shepherds were beautiful, so it was exciting to write about one. I also love writing books that are set in wintertime, since it is my favorite season — even when it's cold and hailing! It was fun to imagine this pure white dog playing in the white snow.

Yours from the Puppy Place,

Ellen Miles

P.S. For another book about a German shepherd, try CHAMP. For other books about dogs who help people, try HONEY, SHADOW, SWEETIE, or TEDDY.

THE PUPPY PLACE

DON'T MISS THE NEXT PUPPY PLACE ADVENTURE!

Here's a peek at Louie

"Over here!" Charles Peterson called to his friend Sammy. "I need your help with this one." He grabbed one end of a huge dead branch—more like a tree, practically!—and tugged as hard as he could. It didn't move.

Sammy trotted over. "That's a big one," he said, looking down at the branch. "Let's drag it over to the fire pit. It'll make awesome firewood for the party later on."

It was a chilly day in May. A few patches of blue polka-dotted the mostly gray sky. Charles and Sammy, and the rest of their Cub Scout pack, were busy helping clean up Loon Lake Park for the summer season. When they were done, their families would meet them there and they would celebrate with the first cookout of the year.

Charles and Sammy were on the "pick-up" team. Their job was to pick up any branches or twigs that had fallen over the winter. Other teams were gathering trash, raking, and hauling the raked leaves to a big pile.

Charles didn't mind the work. It was fun to be at the park before the official opening day. In a few weeks, there would be kids racing around the playground, noisy volleyball games, and swimmers and kayakers splashing in the water. Now, everything was quiet and peaceful. The grass was just starting to turn green, the leaves on the trees were tender and new, and the colorful canoes and kayaks were still piled on shore, waiting for their first voyages across the lake.

Springtime at Loon Lake Park was special, but Charles also liked being there in the middle of winter, when his family had a tradition of having a picnic each year. It was even quieter then, when snow covered the grassy areas and thick ice trapped the sparkling waters of the lake.

Charles would never forget the winter day when his family had seen a puppy fall through the ice. That had been so scary, but with the help of a special cold-water rescue team they had saved the curly-haired pup. Noodle had become one of the Petersons' favorite foster puppies as they tried to find out where he belonged. Lizzie,

Charles's older sister, had become especially attached to Noodle and had a hard time saying good-bye to him when the time came. But that was what fostering was all about: The Petersons only kept each puppy long enough to find him or her the perfect forever home. Even the Bean, Charles's younger brother, understood that.

"Remember Noodle?" Charles asked Sammy now, as they dragged the big branch toward the ring of stones near the sandy beach. It was slow going, but with both of them pulling hard they could keep moving.

"Of course," said Sammy. "I remember every single one of your foster puppies."

ABOUT THE AUTHOR

Ellen Miles loves dogs, which is why she has a great time writing the Puppy Place books. And guess what? She loves cats, too! (In fact, her very first pet was a beautiful tortoiseshell cat named Jenny.) That's why she came up with the Kitty Corner series. Ellen lives in Vermont and loves to be outdoors with her dog, Zipper, every day, walking, biking, skiing, or swimming, depending on the season. She also loves to read, cook, explore her beautiful state, play with dogs, and hang out with friends and family.

Visit Ellen at www.ellenmiles.net.